wind flyers

BY ANGELA JOHNSON   ILLUSTRATED BY LOREN LONG

Simon & Schuster Books for Young Readers

New York   London   Toronto   Sydney

Great-great-uncle was a wind flyer.

A smooth wind flyer.
A Tuskegee wind flyer. . . .

His whole life
all he *ever* wanted to do was fly.

With his arms flapping,
he jumped off a chicken coop
when he was five.

Then jumped off a barn
into soft hay
when he was seven.

Uncle says it's 'cause he'd watched
some birds fly that day.

When he was eleven,
he paid seventy-five cents to
go up with a flying barnstormer.

"It's what heaven must be,"
Uncle says to me.
"With clouds, like soft blankets, saying,
'Come on in, get warm.
Stay awhile and be a
wind flyer too.'"

They flew over the fields,
over the lakes,

and Uncle just knew
if he could get a good grip,
those clouds would be his. . . .

He cried when they landed
because then he knew
what it was like to go
into the wind,

  against the wind,

beyond the wind.

"There was magic in the wind back then," he says.

When he was older,
Uncle became a Tuskegee Airman with the 332nd.
He studied hard and flew in a war.

"Air Force didn't want us at first.
Only four squadrons like us," he says,
touching his mahogany face.

And when his plane left the red Alabama dirt
and flew in the air,
he hoped he would never come down.

He had finally become a wind flyer,
a smooth wind flyer,
a Tuskegee wind flyer.
Flying high above it all;
never to touch the earth again.

Forever a wind flyer.

When I ask him if it was a big war, Uncle says. "They all are. But that's over now. . . ."

"We were something. Some of us didn't come back,
but we never lost a plane we protected."

Then Uncle points at the picture of him
and the wind flyers,
those smooth wind flyers,
those Tuskegee wind flyers.

"Young and brave. Brave and young, all."

Uncle crop dusted some,
right after the war.
That's the only way he could still fly,
the only way he could still catch the clouds
and feel the wind.

He says flying is different now, though.

Faster planes.
More people than ever.

But Uncle says the clouds
still sound the same.

He holds my hand,
and we watch new wind flyers
jet through the clouds.

Then once in a while, he takes me up
and we become the smooth wind flyers

Tuskegee wind flyers

flying into the wind,

against the wind,

beyond the wind,

the magical wind.

For Sidney Perlman
—A. J.

To Paul,
for sharing your love of planes, trains, and the stars
—L. L.

AUTHOR'S NOTE

In January of 1941, under pressure from the NAACP and other groups, the U.S. Army Air Force created the all-black 99th Pursuit Squadron. The 332nd Fighter Group had been formed in 1942, making it the only four-squadron fighter group in the Army Air Force. These pilots were trained on an airfield in Tuskegee, Alabama, and thus called, the Tuskegee Airmen; although the army had no intention of ever using them in battle. Under pressure from the Roosevelt administration the 99th was finally posted in North Africa in 1943. The segregated squadron eventually turned out six hundred pilots and 145,000 support personnel, and they earned numerous distinguished flying awards and unit citations. The 332nd distinguished themselves as the only escort group that never lost a single bomber to enemy fire.

SIMON & SCHUSTER BOOKS FOR YOUNG READERS • An imprint of Simon & Schuster Children's Publishing Division • 1230 Avenue of the Americas, New York, New York 10020 • Text copyright © 2007 by Angela Johnson • Illustrations copyright © 2007 by Loren Long • All rights reserved, including the right of reproduction in whole or in part in any form. • SIMON & SCHUSTER BOOKS FOR YOUNG READERS is a trademark of Simon & Schuster, Inc. • Book design by Dan Potash • The text for this book is set in Barbera. • The illustrations for this book are rendered in acrylic paint. • Manufactured in China

2   4   6   8   10   9   7   5   3   1

CIP data for this book is available from the Library of Congress.

ISBN-13: 978-0-689-84879-7

ISBN-10: 0-689-84879-X